Published by Pleasant Company Publications
© Copyright 2001 by Pleasant Company
All rights reserved. No part of this book may be used or reproduced in
any manner whatsoever without written permission except in the case of
brief quotations embodied in critical articles and reviews.
For information, address: Book Editor, Pleasant Company Publications,
8400 Fairway Place, P.O. Box 620998, Middleton, WI 53562.

Printed in Singapore.
01 02 03 04 05 06 07 08 TWP 10 9 8 7 6 5 4 3 2 1

The American Girls Collection® and logo, American Girls Short Stories,™
the American Girl logo, Josefina,® and Josefina Montoya®
are trademarks of Pleasant Company.

Edited by Nancy Holyoke and Michelle Jones
Designed by Joshua Mjaanes and Laura Moberly
Art Directed by Joshua Mjaanes

Library of Congress Cataloging-in-Publication Data

Tripp, Valerie, 1951-
Josefina's song / by Valerie Tripp ;
illustrations, Jean-Paul Tibbles ; vignettes, Susan McAliley.
p. cm. — (The American girls collection)
Summary: In the early 1800s, ten-year-old Josefina accompanies
her father into the New Mexican mountains to check on the elderly
shepherd who works for him, and she proves herself a good traveling
companion when her father has an accident.

ISBN 1-58485-272-0
[1. Mexican Americans—Fiction. 2. Shepherds—Fiction.
3. New Mexico—Fiction.]
I. Tibbles, Jean-Paul, ill. II. McAliley, Susan, ill. III. Title. IV. Series.
PZ7.T7363 Jpr 2001   [Fic]—dc21   00-032650

The
AMERICAN GIRLS
COLLECTION
®

OTHER AMERICAN GIRLS
SHORT STORIES:

FELICITY TAKES A DARE

KIRSTEN SNOWBOUND!

ADDY'S WEDDING QUILT

SAMANTHA AND THE
MISSING PEARLS

MOLLY MARCHES ON

PICTURE CREDITS

The following organizations have generously given
permission to reprint illustrations contained in "Looking Back":
p. 34—Copyright Michael Heller, "Las Carneradas" by John O. Baxter,
University of New Mexico Press, 1987; p. 35—Churro with horns,
photo by Robert Nymeyer, courtesy Museum of New Mexico, neg. no. 59014;
p. 37—From the book *Trajes Civiles, Militares y Religiosos de Mexico* by
Claudio Linati (1828); p. 38—Christine Preston; p. 39—"Shearing a sheep in the
traditional way at el Rancho de las Golondrinas, La Cienega, New Mexico,"
photo by Nancy Hunter Warren from *Villages of Hispanic New Mexico*,
copyright 1987 by Nancy Hunter Warren, School of American Research,
Santa Fe; p. 40—Photography by Jamie Young, prop styling by Jean doPico,
and craft by Judith Mjaanes.

TABLE OF CONTENTS

JOSEFINA'S FAMILY

PAPÁ
Josefina's father, who guides his family and his rancho with quiet strength.

ANA
Josefina's oldest sister, who is married and has two little boys.

JOSEFINA
A ten-year-old girl whose heart and hopes are as big as the New Mexico sky.

FRANCISCA
Josefina's sixteen-year-old sister, who is headstrong and impatient.

CLARA
Josefina's practical, sensible sister, who is thirteen years old.

TÍA DOLORES
*Josefina's aunt, who
lives with Josefina's
family on their rancho.*

SANTIAGO
*The shepherd at
the Montoyas' camp in
the mountains.*

ANGELITO
*Santiago's nine-year-old
grandson.*

Josefina and her family speak
Spanish, so you'll see some Spanish
words in this book. If you can't tell
what a word means from reading the
story or looking at the illustrations,
you can turn to the "Glossary of
Spanish Words" on page 48. It will
tell you what the word means and
how to pronounce it.

Remember that in Spanish, "j"
is pronounced like "h." That means
Josefina's name is pronounced
"ho-seh-FEE-nah."

JOSEFINA'S SONG

Josefina kicked off her moccasins and waded into the stream. The water swirled around her legs. It felt silky and cold. She scooped up some to drink, then patted her cheeks with her wet hands.

"I wish I were one of Papá's sheep," she said to her sisters, who were washing clothes. "Then I'd spend the summer in the mountains, where it's cool."

Ana and Clara laughed. But Francisca bleated like a sheep. "Baa!" she said.

"Who cares about the mountains? *I* want to go to Santa Fe next month when the wagon train arrives."

"Me, too!" agreed all the sisters. The wagon train was coming from the United States. The sisters were eager to see the wonderful things like tools, books, buttons, shoes, and beautiful material for dresses that the *americanos* would bring to sell or trade.

"We shouldn't get our hopes up," said Clara, wringing water out of a sock. "Papá hasn't said that he'll take us with him. He has business to do."

The sisters knew Clara was right. Papá was going to Santa Fe to trade mules for sheep. There'd been a terrible flood in the fall, and many sheep were drowned. Papá needed to build up his flock again. Sheep provided meat for eating and wool for weaving and trading. The *rancho* couldn't survive without them.

"I'm sure Papá will take us," Josefina said cheerfully. "And he'll trade his mules for hundreds of sheep. It will be just like in the shepherds' song." She sang:

> *Happy shepherds,*
> *goodness has triumphed!*
> *Heaven has opened!*
> *Life has been born.*

When she finished, Josefina was surprised to see that Papá had come to the stream. "You sing that song beautifully, child," he said.

"*Gracias*, Papá," said Josefina, blushing at his praise. "The shepherd Santiago taught it to me."

"Ah, yes," said Papá. "Santiago and his grandson Angelito are your friends, aren't they?"

"*Sí*," said Josefina, "though I see them only in the winter." During the warm months, Santiago and Angelito lived up in the mountains, tending part of Papá's flock. "Santiago loves living on the mountain. He said that he and Angelito would rather be there than anywhere else on earth. But I do miss them."

"Well," said Papá, "I'm going to visit them tomorrow. I heard that Santiago was ill. I want to be sure he's better.

Would you like to come, too?"

"Oh, sí, Papá!" said Josefina with all her heart.

"Good," said Papá. "We'll leave early in the morning."

He turned to go, but Francisca stepped forward. "Pardon me, Papá," she said. "Since you are speaking of traveling, I thought I might ask, have you decided if my sisters and I may go to Santa Fe with you next month?"

"I haven't decided," Papá said. "I'll see how well Josefina does on our trip up the mountain tomorrow."

The second Papá was gone, Francisca spun around and demanded, "Josefina, did you hear what Papá said?"

Francisca spun around and demanded, "Josefina,
did you hear what Papá said?"

6

"Yes!" said Josefina joyfully. "I'm going to see my friends! I'll sing with Santiago. Angelito and I—"

"Not *that!*" Francisca cut in. "I meant what Papá said about watching you. Your trip tomorrow will be a test. You must behave perfectly. Don't be any trouble. Don't slow Papá down. Don't complain about being tired or hungry or thirsty."

"I won't," said Josefina. "I'll sing all the way."

"No! Don't!" said Clara. "Be quiet! Don't annoy Papá or you'll ruin our chances of going to Santa Fe."

"And if you do," said Francisca, "we'll never speak to you again!"

"Don't worry," said Josefina, grinning.

7

"I'll be perfect. After all, I want to go to Santa Fe as much as you do."

❋

It was easy for Josefina to follow Francisca's advice. Even after she and Papá had been riding for hours, Josefina was too delighted by all she was seeing to be tired or hungry or thirsty. But it was *not* easy to be quiet. Josefina wanted to sing along with the wind, chirp back to the birds, and ask Papá hundreds of questions. But she remembered Clara's advice and never made a sound.

"You're so quiet," Papá said as they stopped to let the horses drink from the stream.

"I'd expected my little bird to be singing all morning. Is the ride too hard for you?"

"No, Papá!" Josefina exclaimed quickly.

"Good," said Papá. "Anyway, it's not much longer now."

In a few minutes, Papá and Josefina heard the clear, high sound of Santiago's flute. As they rode into the little clearing, Josefina saw Santiago sitting by the fire outside his tent. He had a lamb in his lap.

"*Buenos días*, Santiago," Papá called out. "God be with you."

"Is that you, *patrón*?" said Santiago, standing up.

"Sí, and my daughter Josefina," said Papá as they got off their horses.

"*Señorita* Josefina!" said Santiago.

"Welcome!"

"Gracias, Santiago," said Josefina, smiling at her friend. But her smile faded when she looked more closely at Santiago's face. His eyes were flat and lifeless. Josefina gasped and quickly looked at Papá. She could tell by his unhappy expression that he'd realized it, too. Santiago was blind! Josefina felt her own eyes fill with tears.

Santiago bowed. "Your visit honors me," he said.

"It is our pleasure," said Papá kindly. He went to Santiago and put his hand on the old man's shoulder. "How are you?" he asked.

"By God's grace, my illness is over,"

said Santiago. "I'm as strong as ever. But my sight is gone. I am blind."

"I'm sorry," said Papá. Josefina saw a look of deep concern on his face. Then he asked, "Where is Angelito?"

"He's with the sheep," said Santiago. "He watches the flock now while I tend our camp." Santiago picked up the lamb that had been in his lap. "I care for the sheep that are hurt, or sick, or orphaned like this fellow."

"A shepherd's life is not easy. There's much to do," said Papá, patting the lamb. He turned to Josefina. "Go tell Angelito I wish to see him."

"Sí, Papá," said Josefina. She hurried up the steep path that led to the pasture.

It felt wonderful to stretch her legs after the long ride.

She was out of breath by the time she saw Angelito. He was near the stream, watching the sheep grazing on its banks. The stream was narrow here, just a swift ribbon of water that slid between the rocks.

"Angelito!" Josefina called.

Angelito looked up and waved. He whistled to the dogs, signaling them to circle the sheep and keep them from wandering. Only when the dogs were in place did he hurry toward Josefina, covering the distance in a few graceful leaps. Angelito was nine years old and small for his age, but he was fast. As he came near, Josefina

saw that his face didn't look as merry as usual.

"Señorita Josefina," Angelito asked, "why are you here?" Then he remembered his manners. "Pardon me," he said. "I meant, buenos días. I hope that you and your family are well."

"By the grace of God, we are," said

Josefina. "My papá has come to see your
grandfather." Josefina paused, then said,
"Oh, Angelito! How long has Santiago
been blind?"

Angelito sighed. "Early this summer
my grandfather was sick with a fever," he
explained. "After the fever went away,
he couldn't see at all." Angelito looked
earnestly at Josefina. "But he doesn't
need to see!" he said. "I can see for him! I
watch the sheep now. The dogs obey me.
I know this mountain better than anyone.
I know all the sheep in our flock, too. I
won't let any of them get lost." He
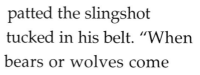
patted the slingshot
tucked in his belt. "When
bears or wolves come

around, I scare them away." Angelito
hesitated, then asked, "Your papá hasn't
. . . he hasn't come to take our flock
away from my grandfather and me, has
he? My grandfather would die if he had
to leave here. The mountains are home
to him. And to me, too."

"My father knows that," said Josefina.
"He would never ask you to leave." But
a tiny, terrible doubt crept into her mind,
and her voice was worried as she said,
"At least, I don't believe he would." She
beckoned to Angelito. "Come, now. He
wants to see you."

Angelito and Josefina went down the
path back to the tent. Santiago was stirring
a spicy-smelling *atolé* stew over the fire

and cooking *tortillas.* Josefina was amazed by how handy he was. Though he could not see, he never faltered or dropped anything as he cooked and served the food. After the meal, Santiago played his flute. The old man's fingers moved quickly, never hitting a wrong note. Angelito's voice blended with the flute in lovely harmony as he sang the *corrido*— a song that he and Santiago had made up about their pleasant, peaceful life on the mountain caring for the sheep and sleeping under the stars.

After the song, Angelito rose to go back to the flock.

"Stay, Angelito," said Papá. He turned to Santiago. "Your song reminds me of the days when I was a boy and you worked for my father and sang your corridos for him," he said. "You've been a faithful servant to my family for many years. I thank you for your loyalty and hard work."

"Bless you, patrón," said Santiago.

"Amigo," said Papá, "I worry for your safety. I'm afraid your blindness makes it dangerous for you to live here, so far from other people. I'm afraid it's dangerous for the sheep, too. A blind shepherd can't keep watch over a flock, and the sheep are too valuable to be entrusted to a child as young as Angelito." Papá's voice was gentle. "I think the time has come for you to rest," he said. "You and Angelito can come live

on the rancho. I'll send another shepherd up here to take over your duties."

Oh, no! thought Josefina. "Don't, Papá!" she burst out passionately. "You mustn't!"

Papá frowned. "My child," he said gravely. "Hold still."

"Papá, I'm sorry. But I must speak," said Josefina. "Santiago and Angelito can care for the flock if they do it together. Angelito is Santiago's eyes. He's a fine shepherd. He's brave and fast and careful! He'll keep the sheep safe, and Santiago will keep them well." Josefina knew she was doing exactly what her sisters had warned her not to do. She was making Papá angry. But she couldn't help it! "Please, Papá," she pleaded. "Don't take their flock away.

You mustn't make them leave the mountain. It's their *home*."

Papá stood. Josefina had seldom seen him look so stern. In a solemn voice he said to Santiago, "I beg you to excuse my daughter's disrespect. I see now that it was a mistake to bring her." Without looking at Josefina, he said, "Wait by the horses."

Josefina did as she was told. When Papá came, she climbed back up on her horse and waved a sad good-bye to her two friends. *What have I done?* she thought as she rode away. *Nothing good. I didn't change Papá's mind. Santiago and Angelito are still going to lose their flock. All I did was make Papá ashamed of me, and so angry that I've surely ruined any chance of going to*

Santa Fe. My sisters will be furious with me!

❋

Josefina, lost in her own dark sorrow, didn't notice that the sky was darkening, too, though it was only midday. After she and Papá had ridden for an hour or so, Josefina felt cold. She shivered, and looked 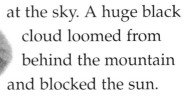 at the sky. A huge black cloud loomed from behind the mountain and blocked the sun. The wind began to blow hard, and then, all in a rush, the rain came. It lashed at Josefina so fiercely that she could hardly see. She pulled her *rebozo* over her head and huddled close to her horse's neck, keeping her eyes fixed on Papá as he rode in front of her. Overhead, the trees swayed crazily in the wind. Underfoot, the path was soon slippery from the rain.

Thunder rumbled in the distance, and then—*crrrack!* A bolt of lightning ripped the sky. With a terrified squeal, Papá's horse reared up. Its hooves pawed the air wildly. To her horror, Josefina saw Papá fall off his horse and land hard on the rocky ground.

"Papá!" she shrieked. His horse whinnied, then bolted off down the mountain, dragging its reins behind it. Quickly Josefina slid off her horse. "Papá, are you all right?" she asked, kneeling next to him.

"My . . . leg," Papá panted. He tried to sit up, then sank back again, his eyes squeezed shut in pain.

God help me! prayed Josefina, shaking from cold and fear. She knew she had to get Papá to shelter, but where? Home was too far away. Josefina made her voice sound steady. "Papá," she said, "if I help you onto my horse, do you think you can ride back to Santiago's camp?"

Papá nodded. It took all Josefina's strength to help Papá struggle to his feet and mount her horse. When he was settled, she took the reins and started to walk back up the mountain. Again and again she slipped on the rocky path. Again and again her horse stumbled.

The wind raged and the rain fell harder than ever, but Josefina kept on. The stream that had been a thin trickle earlier in the day rushed by now, churning brown and angry.

Then at last, over the noise of the storm and the stream, Josefina heard a shout. She looked up and saw Angelito running toward her.

"My father is hurt!" Josefina called out. "Please, he needs help."

Angelito didn't say a word. He took off his *sarape* and wrapped it around Josefina. Then he took the horse's reins and led the way to the tent.

Josefina crawled inside while Santiago helped Papá off the horse. The sides of the

*The wind raged and the rain fell harder than ever,
but Josefina kept on.*

tent flapped and billowed in the wind, but inside it was dry and cozy. Santiago made Papá comfortable on a bed of sheepskins. Gently, he felt along the bone of Papá's leg.

"A bad sprain," he said. "It's not broken, thank God." Josefina watched as Santiago rubbed ointment on Papá's leg and then carefully, tenderly, made a splint of a blanket and some strips of leather.  "This will hold your leg straight," Santiago said. "It will be as good as new in a few weeks. But you must lie still now, patrón. Rest."

"Gracias, amigo," said Papá. Then he asked, "Where is Angelito?"

"He's taking Josefina's horse to a safe place," said Santiago. "Then he'll keep watch over the sheep to be sure no harm comes to them. He said that he'll stay with them until the storm is over."

Papá nodded. He reached for Josefina's hand, then closed his eyes. But he was restless. Josefina could tell that his leg pained him too much to let him sleep.

"You and I must take his mind off his pain," said Santiago. He took out his flute. "Sing with me," he said, smiling at Josefina.

So Josefina sang. For hours, she sang along with Santiago's flute. She sang all the songs she knew, and then she sang them again. When she ran out of songs, she began to make one up herself. It was

a corrido about her trip up the mountain
with Papá. She sang about her eagerness
to see Santiago and Angelito, about her
outspokenness and Papá's anger, about
the storm, Papá's accident, and at last,
Santiago's comfort and care. She sang
about Angelito's bravery in staying with
the sheep through the rainy night.

Josefina's throat was tired. Her eye-
lids drooped and she ached with sleepi-
ness, but she didn't stop singing. And
deep into the night, Santiago played his
flute for her and for Papá.

❋

When at last the long night was over,
several men from the rancho appeared.
Papá's horse had returned to the stable, so
they'd known right away that something
was wrong and had headed up the
mountain to find Papá and Josefina.

"We are in good hands, as you
can see," Papá said to them.

Santiago built a fire and made
hot tea for everyone. Then

Angelito brought Josefina's horse, and
the men helped Papá and Josefina mount
up and prepare to go back down the
mountain.

Before they left, Papá leaned down
from his horse to shake Santiago's hand.
"Old friend," he said, "thank you for
your help."

"It was my honor," said Santiago.

Papá straightened. "You cared for
me so well," he said. "I know that if any
of my sheep were hurt, you'd care for
them well, too." He turned to Angelito.
"And you, my boy, were as brave and
hardworking last night as any man three
times your age." Papá's voice was seri-
ous. "I spoke hastily when I said that it

was time for you two to come live on the
rancho. I hope you will stay here. I'd be
proud to leave my sheep in your care."

Josefina's heart rose. She smiled at
Angelito, and he smiled back happily.
Santiago bowed and said, "Gracias,
patrón. We'll stay."

Josefina waved good-bye as she and
Papá set off. After they'd gone a short way,
Papá said, "You must be tired, Josefina."

"Oh, no, Papá," said Josefina, even
though she was.

"You were very brave yesterday,"
said Papá. "And I know that you didn't
sleep all night. I heard you singing to
me. I especially liked the corrido you
made up about our adventure on the

mountain." He grinned. "Perhaps when we go to Santa Fe with your sisters, you'll sing that song again."

Josefina laughed aloud with joy and relief. Papá had forgiven her! Tired as she was, she said eagerly, "Sí, Papá, I'll sing it then. I'll sing it now, too." And she did, all the way home.

VALERIE TRIPP

At 9   Now

Oₙe hot, sunny summer day, my family and I were hiking in the mountains near Santa Fe when suddenly, the sky darkened, thunder rumbled, the wind howled, and a cold, hard rain began to fall. *Josefina's Song* is a corrido I made up inspired by our adventure!

Valerie Tripp has written thirty-six books in The American Girls Collection, including nine about Josefina.

Looking
Back
1824

A Peek Into
the Past

Sheep in 1824

The rancho provided almost everything that families like Josefina's needed to live. The sheep on the rancho were especially valued for their meat and wool, used to make warm clothing.

In the 1500s, the Spanish brought the first sheep to

Churro sheep

New Mexico. These small, sturdy sheep called *churros* were used to the dry, mountainous land. Their wool was

Sheepskins were used for the lining of a baby's cradle.

long and thick, which made it good for spinning and dyeing.

Families like the Montoyas owned a few hundred sheep. For most of the year, the family's sheep were kept on the rancho. *Pastores*, or shepherds, like Santiago watched over them. In the summer, when the lower lands became hot and dry, the shepherds took the sheep into the cool mountains.

The shepherds set up camp near a pasture

Many churros had horns pointing in all directions!

and a river or stream. Each morning they herded the sheep to fresh grass. When the sun went down, they herded the sheep back to camp. In the evenings, the shepherds played music on their flutes and told stories. Sometimes they carved animals out of wood.

Often dogs were the only company a shepherd had. The dogs were always on the alert for coyotes, wolves, and bears, and they also helped keep the sheep together. When a sheep strayed too far from the flock, the dog would guide it back, sometimes even nipping the sheep as a warning. At night, the dogs' sheepskin beds were spread out in a protective circle around the flock.

The dogs also protected the sheep if the camp was attacked by Comanche, Apache, or Navajo Indians. These people were *nomadic*, which means

An Apache warrior in 1828

they moved their homes seasonally. Nomadic Indians and New Mexican settlers were enemies. They raided each other's homes, stole animals, and took people captive. If raiders were spotted, shepherds sent the dogs to scatter the flock. But the shepherds knew this would not save all of the sheep—some of them would be stolen.

Guns and ammunition were scarce on the frontier, so a slingshot and stone was usually a shepherd's only weapon. But most shepherds had good aim—they had lots of time to practice shooting at rocks or trees while the sheep grazed.

The shepherds also protected the sheep from bad weather. In the mountains, lightning and floods came on suddenly. They could harm or even kill many sheep in an instant. The shepherds had to act quickly to move the sheep to a safer spot, such as a cave, a woods, or higher ground.

At the end of the summer, the shepherds herded the sheep down from

A flash flood in New Mexico

the mountains to the pastures near the rancho. As winter neared, the sheep were moved closer and closer to the rancho.

In the spring, when the sheep's wool was the thickest, it was time to *shear* the sheep, or shave off their wool. Men used metal shears to cut the sheep's fleeces, one by one. A skilled shearer could cut off a fleece in one piece.

Once the thick coats had been sheared, the sheep were ready for the hot summer. The shepherds moved the sheep back up to the mountains to start the cycle all over again!

An American Girls Pastime

WEAVE A MINI RUG

*Use a simple loom to make
a colorful weaving.*

When Josefina was growing up,
girls and women wove sheep's wool into
colorful blankets and rugs for the rancho.
Josefina's sisters learned how to weave
on the big loom in the weaving room.
Josefina was too small to use this loom,
so she learned on a smaller loom.

Learn to weave just as Josefina might
have. Use a simple cardboard loom to
make a mini rug. Try experimenting with
different colors.

You Will Need:

An adult to help you

*A piece of corrugated cardboard, 5 1/4 x 8 inches
(the corrugation should run vertically)*

Ruler

Pencil

Scissors

String

Yarn of different colors

1. Use the ruler and pencil to mark every ³⁄₈ inch on the short sides of the card-board. Cut a slit at each mark.

Back of Loom

2. Leave about 8 inches of string, then slip the string into the first slit on the bottom-right side of the cardboard. Next slip the string into the first slit on the top-right side.

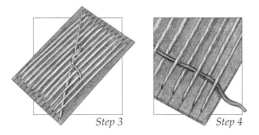

Step 3   *Step 4*

3. Continue wrapping the string around the cardboard until you reach the last slit. Tie the ends of the string together in a knot. This is the back of the loom.

4. Cut a piece of yarn 30 inches long. For row 1, start on the bottom-right side and weave *under,* over, under, over, until you reach the end of the row. Pull the yarn through until only a 1-inch tail is left.

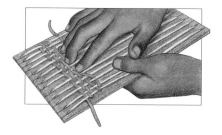

5. For row 2, weave *over*, under, over, under, until the end of the row. Keep weaving new rows. As you weave, keep the yarn loose and use your fingers to push each row close to the one before it.

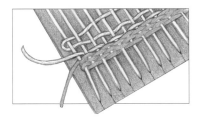

6. To weave in other colors, continue where you left off with the previous color.

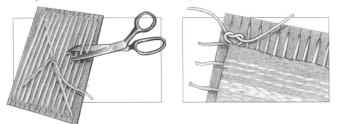

7. When you finish weaving, turn the rug over. Cut 2 strands of string through the middle, and tie them in a double knot at the top and bottom. Repeat until all of the strings have been cut.

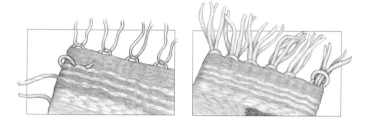

8. Weave the extra yarn ends on the sides of your rug back into the rug. To add extra fringe, tie short pieces of yarn to the string fringes. Unravel the yarn for a fuller fringe.

THE DOVETAIL PATTERN

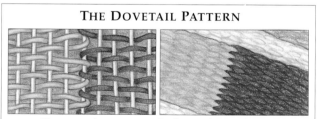

*To weave colors next to each other, or **dovetail**, weave one color halfway across the rug, and then weave it back. Weave another color from the other side in the same way.*

GLOSSARY OF SPANISH WORDS

americanos *(ah-meh-ree-KAH-nohs)*—men from the United States

amigo *(ah-MEE-go)*—friend

atolé *(ah-TOH-leh)*—corn mush or porridge

buenos días *(BWEH-nohs DEE-ahs)*—good morning

churros *(CHOO-rohs)*—small, sturdy sheep

corrido *(koh-REE-doh)*—a song

gracias *(GRAH-see-ahs)*—thank you

pastores *(pahs-TOH-rehs)*—shepherds

patrón *(pah-TROHN)*—a man who has earned respect because he owns land and manages it well, and who is a good leader of his family and his workers

rancho *(RAHN-cho)*—a farm or ranch where crops are grown and animals are raised

rebozo *(reh-BO-so)*—a long shawl worn by girls and women

sarape *(sah-RAH-peh)*—a warm blanket that is wrapped around the shoulders or worn as a poncho

Señorita *(seh-nyo-REE-tah)*—Miss or young lady

sí *(SEE)*—yes

tortillas *(tor-TEE-yahs)*—a kind of flat, round bread made of corn or wheat

BUSINESS REPLY MAIL

FIRST-CLASS MAIL   PERMIT NO. 1137   MIDDLETON WI

POSTAGE WILL BE PAID BY ADDRESSEE

PO BOX 620497
MIDDLETON WI 53562-9940

American Girl ®

Catalogue Request

Add your name and the name of a friend to our mailing list! Simply fill in the names and addresses below and drop this postage-paid card in the mail, visit our Web site at **www.americangirl.com**, or call **1-800-845-0005.**

Send me a catalogue:	Send my friend a catalogue:
My name	My friend's name
Address	Address
City State Zip 1961i	City State Zip 1225i
My birth date: ___/___/___ month day year My e-mail address	
	Parent's signature